Happy 5th Birthday!
♡ with love

Maggie ♡

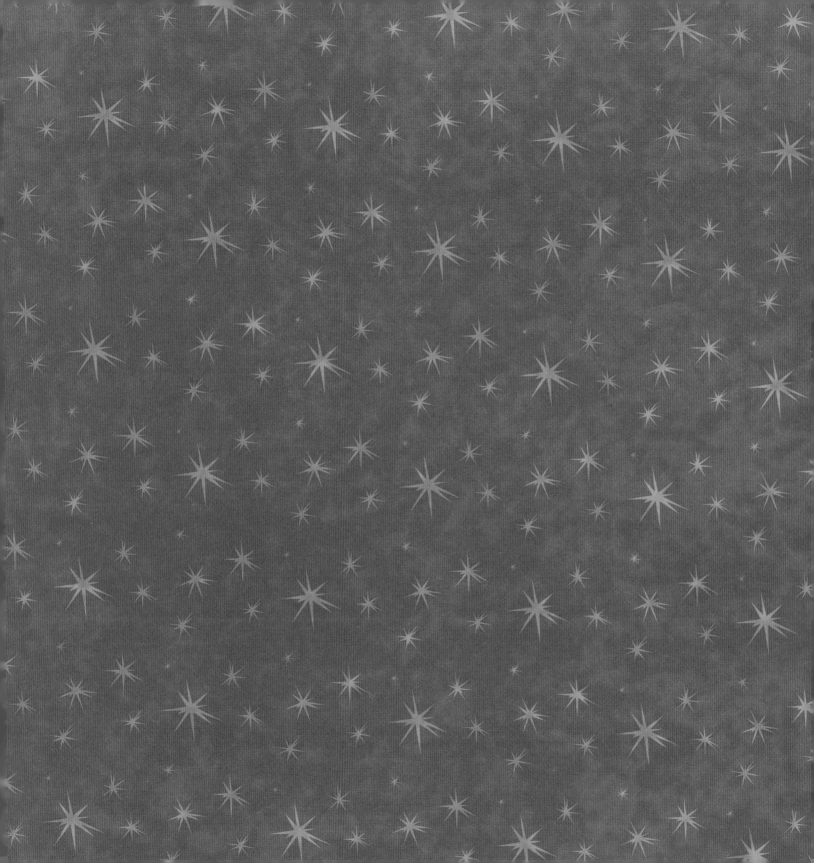

Tink and Friends

STORY COLLECTION

LITTLE, BROWN & COMPANY

LB kids

Little, Brown and Company

Hachette Book Group
237 Park Avenue, New York, NY 10017
Visit our website at lb-kids.com

LB kids is an imprint of Little, Brown and Company.
The LB kids name and logo are trademarks of Hachette Book Group, Inc.

The publisher is not responsible for websites (or their content) that are not owned by the publisher.

First Edition: April 2014
Tinker Bell's Tea Party and *Tinkering Tink* originally published in 2008 by Disney Press, an imprint of Disney Book Group.
Prilla's Prize originally published in 2006 by Disney Press.
Nature's Little Helpers originally published in 2011 by Random House Children's Books, a division of Random House, Inc.
Tinker Bell and the Lost Treasure originally published as *Tiny Adventurers* in 2009 by Random House Children's Books, a division of Random House, Inc.
Fairy Rescue Team originally published in 2010 by Random House Children's Books, a division of Random House, Inc.
A Guide to Pixie Hollow originally published in 2008 by Random House Children's Books, a division of Random House, Inc.

Tinker Bell's Tea Party was written by Lara Bergen and A. Picksey and illustrated by the Disney Storybook Artists.
Prilla's Prize was written by Lisa Papademetriou and illustrated by the Disney Storybook Artists.
Nature's Little Helpers was written by Andrea Posner-Sanchez and illustrated by Caterina Giorgetti and Constance Allen.
Tinkering Tink was written by Elle D. Risco and illustrated by Denise Shimabukuro and Dee Farnsworth.
Tiny Adventurers was adapted by Melissa Arps and illustrated by Emilio Urbano, Manuela Razzi, Jeff Clark, Dave Courtland, William Fenholt, and the Disney Storybook Artists.
Fairy Rescue Team was adapted by Kimberly Morris and illustrated by the Disney Storybook Artists.
A Guide to Pixie Hollow was written by Elle D. Risco and illustrated by Studio IBOIX and the Disney Storybook Artists.

Library of Congress Control Number: 2013957330

ISBN 978-0-316-28336-6

10 9 8 7 6 5 4 3 2 1

WOR

Printed in the United States of America

Contents

Tinker Bell's Tea Party

It was the middle of the morning, and Tinker Bell had finished all her everyday repairs.

She looked around her cozy, cluttered workshop and noticed a piece of shiny Never silver she was saving for a special occasion. There was just enough to make...

"A pretty silver teacup!" Tink said out loud. "Perfect!"

She went to work. Soon enough, Tink had made herself a bright, beautiful teacup. When she tapped it lightly with her hammer, it rang like a bell.

She flew to the tearoom to ask for some tea.

"Tea?" asked Willow, a table-setting fairy.

"Before lunch? Fairy dust! Everyone's so busy;

you will have to make it yourself."

Tinker Bell decided to leave the tearoom and let the table-setting fairies continue their work. But before she left, she grabbed a silver kettle.

Tink took the kettle and flew to a nearby stream for
water. There, she met her friend Rani, a water-talent
fairy. Tink showed Rani the silver cup she had made.
"I am going to make my very own tea," Tink said.

"Oh!" cried Rani. "For a cup that pretty, you should have a special tea—made with morning dew. We can collect some from the flowers in Lily's garden."

Rani led Tinker Bell to Lily's garden, where the flowers still glistened with bright, sweet dew. They were able to collect a few dewdrops from some pink snapdragons. Together, they filled the kettle.

Lily flew over to Tinker Bell and Rani.

"Be careful," she warned. "Sometimes these snapdragons really do snap!"

Lily poked the flowers with a stick to show Tinker Bell and Rani how they bite.

13

At that moment, a snapdragon bent over and nipped at Tinker Bell's hair. Tinker Bell yelped.

Lily hurried over. She stroked the plant's leaves until it let go of Tink's hair.

"You know," Lily said, "four-leaf-clover honey goes perfectly with dewdrop tea." Lily called for her bee friend, Bumble, to lead them to the honey.

Tinker Bell, Rani, and Lily followed Bumble past the orchard and across the marigold meadow. Rani flew on Brother Dove because she does not have wings like the other fairies.

Bumble convinced the bees to give the fairies a generous drop of four-leaf-clover honey. Tink was just about to leave to go start her tea when Beck, an animal-talent fairy, appeared.

"What's the special occasion?" Beck asked.

"Tink is making a special tea with morning dew and four-leaf-clover honey," said Lily.

"What a treat," said Beck. "Are you having lavender cream with it, too?"

"I guess we are off to the dairy farm, fairies!" Tink shouted.

Inside the barn, the fairies collected the lavender cream in flowers and nutshells.

"Okay," Tink said. "I have dew, honey, and plenty of cream. At last I am ready to—"

"Whip the cream!" said Rani. She quickly got to work whipping every drop of cream into fluffy mounds. When Rani was done, she looked around. "That is more than enough."

Tink could hardly wait any longer for her tea.

"Now," Tink said, "I have dew and honey and cream…"

"And huckleberry shortcake," Dulcie said as she walked out of the bakery. "When I heard you were making tea, I couldn't resist making a sweet treat to go with it."

"Now I am more than ready to have a cup of tea," Tink said. "I am ready to have a tea party!"

Linens and decorations fit for a tea party were the only things the fairies didn't have. While some fairies flew to the meadow to collect flowers, Beck flew to the edge of the forest, where the Never spiders weave lace.

"This is perfect!" Beck exclaimed. She picked up lace for a tablecloth and five dainty napkins.

Tinker Bell sat down at the table with her four fairy friends. As she picked up her shiny teacup, the other fairies each raised their teacups in her honor.

"We should say a toast," said Dulcie.

"To whom?" said Tinker Bell.

"To you, Tinker Bell," said Beck. "For bringing us together today—even if you didn't mean to!"

Tinker Bell studied the beautiful teacup she had made that morning. If she had not saved her little piece of Never silver, she would not have had such a fun adventure with her friends.

She tapped the brim of her teacup with her teaspoon.

"To you," she whispered to her teacup. She took a sip of the lovely tea she had been waiting for all day. It was perfect.

Prilla's Prize

"Oh my!" Prilla cried as she raced toward a large field. "I'm late for Great Games Day!"

On this day, all the fairies get together to compete in exciting contests. The fairy that wins first place in each game receives a blue spider-silk ribbon.

Every fairy in Pixie Hollow has a special talent, but Prilla is the only mainland-visiting clapping-talent fairy in all of Never Land. No other fairy has a talent like hers.

Prilla watched as the carpenter-talent fairies added last-minute details to their go-carts, the animal-talent fairies led their birds through a racecourse, and the garden-talent fairies warmed up for the Potato Heft.

"Which contest can I be in?" Prilla wondered aloud.

"Are you going to compete in the games?" asked Rani, a water-talent fairy.

"Yes." Prilla nodded. "But I don't know which one. You see, I'm the only fairy with my talent."

Rani smiled. "That means you can enter any contest you want," she said.

"Attention, garden fairies!"
an announcing-talent fairy called.
"The Potato Heft is about to begin!
Whoever can lift the largest potato
will win!"

Lily was the first to lift a very large
potato into the air. As Lily set the potato
down, the other garden-talent fairies clapped.

"I can lift a potato!" Prilla said.

Prilla walked over to the potato that Lily had lifted. She grabbed
hold and lifted with all her might, but the potato didn't move! She
could only lift a very tiny potato.

Next, the garden-talent fairies lined up for the Carrot Toss. Whoever could throw a carrot the farthest would win! Prilla chose a baby carrot. Lifting it up, she threw it as hard as she could.

Plop!

Prilla's carrot landed two inches away from her. Beside her, Thistle, a garden-talent fairy, launched a giant carrot. It soared through the air and landed point-down in the dirt.

"Fifteen asparagus lengths!" the judge cried. "Thistle is the winner!"

"You gave it a good try, Prilla," Lily said.

Moving on from the garden-talent fairies, Prilla flew back toward the main field. As she passed a tall tree, she caught sight of an obstacle course.

"That must be for the fast-flying fairies," Prilla said to herself. She decided to take a closer look at the course.

"I see," she said. "Over and under the spiderwebs, then hop in and out of the pots, and finish around the pinecones. Hmm... I think I can do it!"

"Prilla, darling, whatever are you doing here?" asked Vidia with a sneer. "This race is for fast-flying fairies, dear, and you certainly aren't a fast flier."

"I can still try," Prilla said.

"Suit yourself." Vidia shrugged and went to the starting line.

Prilla's heart thumped as she lined up next to Vidia and the other fast-flying fairies. *I hope I win this race*, she thought.

"On your marks..." the announcer called. "Get set..." He blew on a reed whistle.

Prilla sprang into the air! But the other fairies were faster. As they dashed forward, their powerful wings sent up a huge gust of wind, knocking Prilla back. She tumbled down, down, down.

Prilla was upset about losing three competitions. She decided to take a break and go to the stream.

"Prilla!" Rani said. "You're just in time. Come join the Leaf Boat Race."

Prilla looked at the leaf boats lined up at the edge of the water. She still wanted to win a blue ribbon.

"I didn't mean to join the boat race," Prilla admitted. "But now that I'm here, I'd love to try it!"

Prilla swam to nearby land to shake her wet wings. She was standing on the edge of a long green lawn dotted with pots and pans turned on their sides.

Clang! A dried pea rattled into a saucepan.

"Good shot, Tinker Bell!" called a fairy.

Smiling, Tinker Bell twirled her ladle over her shoulder. Then she saw Prilla, soaked from the boat race. "What happened to you?" she asked.

Prilla blushed. "I fell into the stream," she explained.

"Why don't you try Ladle Croquet? You can borrow my ladle," Tink offered.

Prilla took Tink's ladle and aimed at a pea. Her hit sent the pea flying far into the woods. She had to go find it. She searched under mushrooms and peered inside mouseholes. Finally, she found the pea in a patch of bluebells.

"I found it!" Prilla raced back to the lawn. But the game was already over.

Prilla sighed. It looked like she wasn't going to win a ribbon for Ladle Croquet, either.

Prilla looked around the great lawn, but all the games were over.
She began to cry. She was never going to win a blue ribbon now.

"Prilla, what's wrong?" asked a soft voice.

Looking up, Prilla saw Rani and Tinker Bell.

"I entered so many contests," Prilla explained, "but I didn't win
anything. I didn't even come close."

Rani turned to Tink and whispered in her ear. With a smile, Tink turned to another fairy and whispered in her ear. Soon, all the fairies were whispering.

"What's going on?" Prilla asked.

"Prilla, everyone agrees that you've set a new record," Tink announced. She took off her ribbon and pinned it to Prilla's dress. "In honor of the most games ever tried, I present this ribbon to you," she said.

The fairies burst into applause.

Prilla blushed with pride. She had won after all.

Nature's Little Helpers

Fairies of all different talents work together to bring the seasons to Pixie Hollow.

Tinker Bell and her fairy friends make the icicles glisten in the winter and the flowers blossom in the springtime. They encourage the birds to sing songs in the summer, and they work together to change the colors of the leaves in the fall.

The fairies love bringing the different seasons to Pixie Hollow. In the summer, the fairies must take care of the animals in the hot sun.

Beck, an animal-talent fairy, makes sure the bunnies have plenty of carrots. Tinker Bell helps feed carrots to a rabbit.

Silvermist, a water-talent fairy, collects waterdrops in a nutshell to give to the thirsty rabbit after her meal.

During the winter, when daylight is shorter, Iridessa catches sunbeams in a bucket and gives the light to the fireflies. Their bright bottoms help light up Pixie Hollow at night—no electricity required!

In the spring and summer, the fireflies are able to collect and store enough sunlight themselves.

During the winter, water is frozen in the cold. Silvermist and the other fairies know how important water is all year long. They often venture around Pixie Hollow to collect dewdrops to use for washing, cooking, and drinking throughout the year.

In the cold weather, animals, like the hedgehog, must hibernate to keep warm and survive the winter.

Fawn takes care of the animals. She is an animal-talent fairy. If a hedgehog is having trouble falling asleep, Fawn comes to the rescue with a handmade dandelion-fluff pillow.

During both the fall and spring, Rosetta plants flowers,
vegetables, and fruits for the fairies of Pixie Hollow to enjoy.
In the fall, they can pick pumpkins, while during the spring,
they have plenty of delicious fruits to eat and pretty flowers to pick.

When all the leaves change colors and fall to the ground, the fairies must find a way to collect them.

Luckily, Tinker Bell is a great tinkerer! She loves to find Lost Things and discover new ways to use them. She finds a harmonica and a glove and ties them together with a piece of vine to make a handy vacuum cleaner!

On especially hot days in the summer, the fairies are happy to have Vidia around. She is a fast-flying fairy and can make big breezes to cool down the fairies in Pixie Hollow.

As the seasons change, the fairies don't let anything go to waste. They gather acorns from the forest floor and remove their caps. Then they use the caps as cups and bowls!

Tink and Terence love to eat strawberry shortcake with cherries in their acorn-cap bowls!

The fairies also reuse other materials found in Pixie Hollow. Their dresses are handmade from flowers, petals, leaves, and moss!

Rosetta tries on a pretty purple-and-pink dress made with petals and leaves.

The seasons continue to change each year in Pixie Hollow.
Luckily, the fairies help out by using their wonderful talents.
They are nature's little helpers!

Tinkering Tink

It was early one morning in the enchanted land of Pixie Hollow. Lily, a garden-talent fairy, hurried over to her friends Tink and Beck to ask if one of them would water her garden that day while she was away.

"Sorry, Lily," said Beck, an animal-talent fairy. "I've got to look after some young Never frogs. They're very fussy."

"I can do it," Tink said with a shrug. She wasn't busy.

Tink had never watered plants before. But how hard could it be, anyway?

Lily showed Tink where to find the watering cans, how to fill them at the well, and how much water to sprinkle on each flower.

"And that's all there is to it!" Lily said.

Tink started watering the flowers. She carefully sprinkled just the right amount of water over each plant.

"This is boring," Tink said. Row after row of flowers stretched out before her. "This is going to take forever!"

Suddenly, Tinker Bell had a tinker-ific idea! She could invent a machine that would do the watering *for* her!

She used a long vine to string the watering cans above the flowers. She secured the end of the vine to a sturdy sunflower stalk. Next she grabbed the other end tightly and flew in circles, watering all the flowers at once!

Tink was done watering in
no time!

"As long as I'm here," she
said to herself, "what else needs
tending?"

She looked around the garden. In a hot, sunny corner, she spotted flowers with a few yellowing leaves.

"They were just watered," she said. "Maybe they need a bit of shade."

Quick as a wink, tinkering
Tink had created a rotating
shade from a twig and three
large flower leaves.

"There!" she said. "Now the flowers can take turns getting out of the strong sun."

But Tink wasn't done yet. One after another, ideas popped into her head—ideas for making Lily's gardening work faster, easier, and better!

Every gardener should have contraptions to water, shade, hoe, and plant seeds, Tink thought. *Or...one contraption that can do it all!*

Tink fetched her tools and all the parts she would need. Then she got to work.

When Lily returned to the garden that afternoon, she found Tink testing her masterpiece. It watered. It shaded. It hoed, and it planted! It was a...

"Gardening machine!" Tink announced proudly to Lily.

Lily watched, speechless, as Tink showed her how it worked.

"Tink, thank you," Lily said. She paused, choosing her words carefully. "The garden looks beautiful. It's a wonderful invention. But, well, I like to water and plant seeds—by hand. To me, it's really... exciting!"

Tink felt disappointed. She had worked so hard on her machine. Suddenly, she heard a chorus of eager peeping and a familiar voice coming from the other side of some tall reeds. She flew over to find...

...Beck! Tink's friend was surrounded by unhappy little frogs, each peeping for her attention.

"Tink!" Beck cried. "I'm so glad to see you! I just don't know what to do with these Never frogs. Some of them are too dry, some of them are too hot, and the rest want to be fed—all at once! I can't keep up!"

Tink had an idea. She hurried back to her gardening machine and pushed it to the bank of the stream.

Soon enough, the machine was sprinkling water over some frogs, creating cool shade for others, and feeding a steady stream of Never fruit seeds to the rest.

"You're a genius, Tink!" Beck said.

Tink beamed with satisfaction. Her all-in-one gardening machine turned out to be perfect for taking care of baby frogs! It couldn't have worked better if she had planned it that way!

Maybe, just for the time being, Tink would pretend that she had.

Tinker Bell
and the
Lost Treasure

Tinker Bell was getting ready for an adventure to the lost island north of Never Land. She wrote down everything she needed to bring on her trip.

She needed her map, a compass, food, pixie dust, sticks, and her pots and pans. She gathered all her things and headed out.

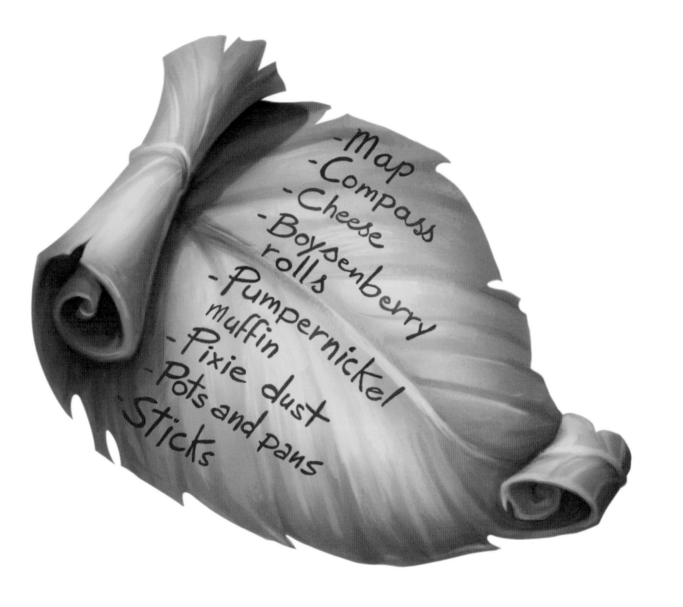

For her big trip, Tink realized she needed a mode of transportation! She built a cotton-ball balloon powered by pixie dust to take her on her long journey from Pixie Hollow.

She set sail. Night was coming, and soon it would be dark out.

As soon as it became dark, Tinker Bell's balloon was knocked by a swarm of fireflies. A speedy bat had been chasing the fireflies!

Tink steered the balloon to keep it steady. She lost the bat, and the fireflies were safe.

One firefly, Blaze,
wanted to join her on her
journey to Never Land.

"Blaze," Tink said. "I could use some help reading my map in the dark!"

Tinker Bell pulled out her map to make sure she was still on track. Blaze buzzed over to help her read in the dark.

"You are a good little friend to have on my journey," Tink said. Blaze smiled. He loved helping others.

The next morning, Tinker Bell and Blaze ran into trouble. It was a very cold and windy day. Tink tried to control the balloon, but the wind swept it away. She lost the balloon, her compass, her pixie dust, and the rest of her supplies.

"What are we going to do now?" she yelled.

Blaze was worried, but he knew he could depend on his insect friends to help once they landed.

Blaze's friends gave Tinker Bell and Blaze food and water. While they rested, they quenched their thirst with fresh dew and ate delicious honey.

"Thank you all!" Tink said. "Blaze, you are so lucky to have such wonderful and generous friends."

Blaze nodded in agreement. He was a very lucky firefly.

They hugged Blaze's friends good-bye and headed into the night.

They reached a tunnel and had to pass through it. But inside, there were two trolls guarding the tunnel's exit.

Tinker Bell and Blaze quietly sneaked past the two arguing trolls.

"That was close," Tink whispered. "I thought they were going to turn around at any moment and grab us!"

They continued down the dark and spooky tunnel. Tinker Bell was worried about Blaze making so much noise with his buzzing.

She removed her leaf headband and wrapped it around Blaze. Now she could use him as a flashlight and keep him quiet!

Suddenly, Tink and Blaze heard a yelp coming from the end of the tunnel. It sounded like their friend Terence!

"Help!" Terence cried. "I am surrounded by a pack of rats!"

Tink ran with Blaze to the end
of the tunnel to save Terence. Using
Blaze's light, she cast a shadow on
the wall that looked like a large, scary
monster. Instantly, the rats were
scared away and Terence was safe.

Tinker Bell, Terence, and Blaze agreed that this was a very exciting adventure, but it was time to head home! They hopped back in the balloon and set sail for Pixie Hollow.

They were happy to leave the bats, trolls, and rats behind.

"I can't wait to be back in Pixie Hollow!" Tink shouted.

Back in Pixie Hollow, Tink and Blaze were happy to be home. They waved good-bye to Terence. Tinker Bell could not wait for her next adventure.

Even though she is small, no adventure is too big for Tink, especially when she has great friends by her side!

Fairy Rescue Team

The fairies were on the mainland for the summer season change. Tinker Bell and Vidia were off exploring when Vidia suddenly came running into the fairy camp. "Tinker Bell's been captured by humans!" she cried.

"What?" The others gasped.

All of Tink's friends—Silvermist, Fawn, Rosetta, Iridessa, Clank, and Bobble—gathered around Vidia.

"Tinker Bell went into this little house in the meadow and couldn't get back out," Vidia told the others.

The "little house" Vidia was talking about was a fairy house built by a human girl named Lizzy. The girl had hoped it would attract a curious fairy like Tinker Bell. And it had!

Vidia realized she couldn't save Tink by herself. A storm was coming, and she needed help.

Tinker Bell's friends started planning a rescue. The rain made it impossible for them to fly—water makes fairy wings too heavy. They built a boat out of bark and reeds.

If they couldn't fly to the rescue, they would sail to the rescue.

It was a dangerous journey. Floodwaters swirled around them. Fawn climbed to the top of the mast to see what was ahead.

"Oh no!" she shouted. They were headed straight for a waterfall. If they went over, they would crash into the rocks below!

Silvermist, a water fairy, knew just what to do. "Rosetta, come grab my feet," she said.

With Rosetta holding on to her ankles, Silvermist leaned out of the boat and touched the raging water with her fingertips.

Using all her water-fairy magic and strength, Silvermist made a water bridge. The fairies held on tight as the boat shot down a new path of water, avoiding the waterfall. It was a wild ride!

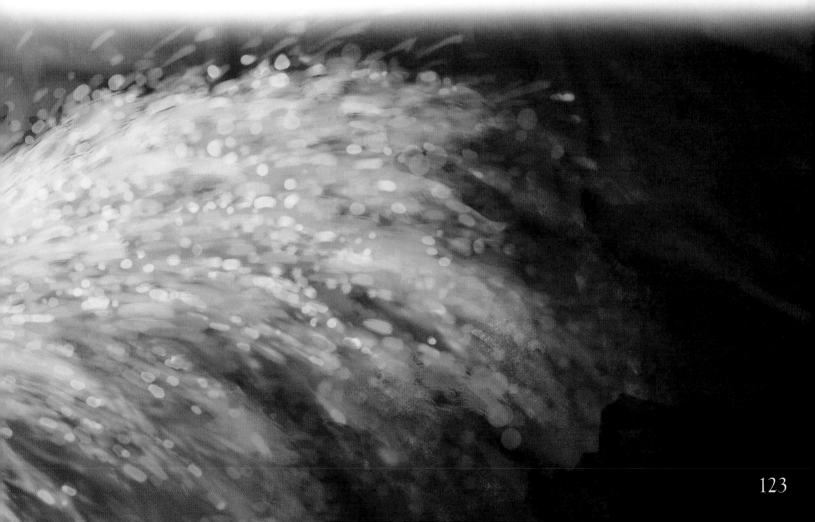

The boat crashed into a bank of tall weeds. None of the fairies were injured, but the boat was destroyed!

"Looks like we're walking from here," Vidia said.

"But walking where?" Fawn asked.

"There's no way of knowing which way to go," Clank moaned.

The fairies were lost!

Just then, Vidia looked at the ground and saw a trail of buttons—the same buttons that had first led her and Tinker Bell to the fairy house.

"I know where we are!" Vidia announced happily.

Vidia led the group through the high grass to a road.
But the road was flooded. She bravely jumped and landed
in muddy water up to her ankles.

"It's not deep," she said. "We can walk across."

One by one, the fairies walked through the icky mud.
But when it was Rosetta's turn, she shook her head.

"I don't really do mud," she told them.

"But you're a garden fairy," Vidia argued.

Rosetta realized she had no choice. She took off her sandals and stepped daintily across. "Ew! Squishy!" she complained.

127

As the group got closer to their destination, Vidia grew more worried. She had a secret she needed to share with the fairies.

"Listen, there's something you all should know," she said. "Tinker Bell getting trapped is my fault."

Vidia admitted that she had slammed the door of the little house shut with Tink inside and wasn't able to open it again. "Now I've put us all in danger. I am so sorry."

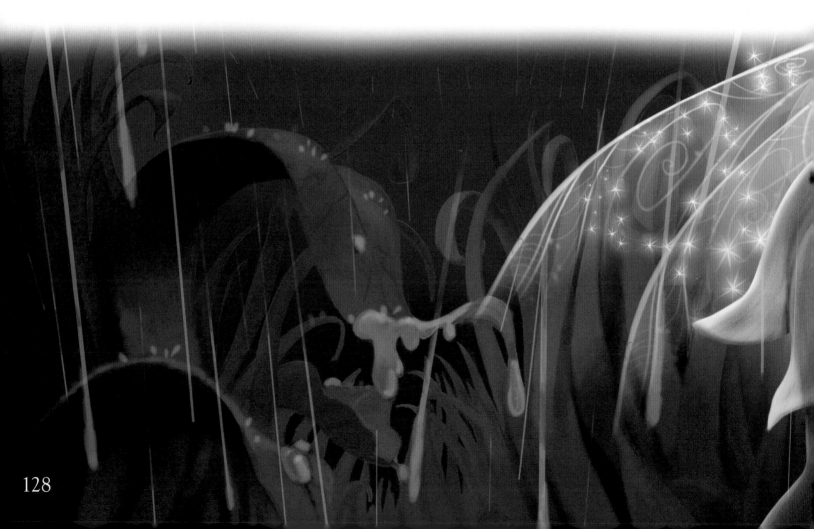

The fairies told her not to worry; she was doing the right thing now. The fairies were glad to have Vidia as part of the team. As a group, they would save Tink.

They put their hands together and recited their special pledge.

"Faith, trust, and pixie dust," they all said.

The fairies kept moving through the dark and rainy night. When they reached the house where Lizzy lived, they sneaked into the kitchen. Vidia told them to be very careful. Not only did they need to watch out for the little girl and her father, but they also needed to watch out for a cat.

"Cat?" Iridessa gasped. "What cat?"

"That cat!" Clank and Bobble wailed.

Just then, the cat, Mr. Twitches, came in. He was wet. And he was angry. The fairies backed into a corner, and Mr. Twitches pounced!

The fairies scattered in every direction. Clank landed on a shelf and sprinkled pixie dust over all the cups and saucers.

The dishes floated into the air, and the fairies jumped aboard, spinning around the kitchen. Then Fawn spotted a plant on the windowsill. "Rosetta, is this what I think it is?"

"Darling, that's exactly what you think it is—catnip!"

133

Clever Fawn used all her animal-fairy magic—plus a little bit of the catnip—to tame Mr. Twitches. A few whiffs turned him into a real pussycat. Everybody climbed aboard the happy kitty and prepared to find Tinker Bell.

But they didn't have to go far...

...because at that moment, Tink came into the kitchen with Lizzy.

"Tinker Bell!" the fairies shouted.

The rescue was a success! The fairies knew that, after the rain stopped, it was going to be a wonderful summer—not just for them, but also for Lizzy, the little girl who believed in fairies.

A Guide to Pixie Hollow

Tinker Bell wants to take you on a tour of the wonderful Pixie Hollow! "Close your eyes and imagine a magical land...." Tinker Bell says.

Pixie Hollow is a land where fairies use their special talents and a bit of pixie dust to put the finishing touches on nature. Flowers are painted by hand, snowflakes are individually frozen, rainbows are spun from water and sunshine—and all four seasons exist at once!

How does a fairy get to this tiny wonderland, you ask? "It's easy!" Tink shouts. "Just take flight, and follow the second star to the right. Ride the breeze, cross the sea, and before you know it, there you are."

Each fairy in Pixie Hollow is born from a human baby's first laugh. The laugh arrives in Pixie Hollow, and with a sprinkling of pixie dust, the fairy comes to life. Fairies also discover their talents on their very first day in Pixie Hollow.

Welcome to Tinker Bell's house! Like every fairy's home, Tink's is special in its own way. From her house, she has a great view of the tinker fairies' village. She can see her friends' houses, too—Silvermist, Rosetta, Iridessa, and Fawn.

Rosetta

Silvermist

Iridessa

Fawn

"I am a tinker fairy," says Tink. "I love to invent things. I am also very determined, curious, and sometimes a bit impatient."

Lilypad Pond is the peaceful home of the water fairies. The sounds of lapping streams and tiny waterfalls are relaxing and musical. While touring the pond by leaf boat, you might see water fairies collecting dewdrops from spiderwebs or sculpting water like clay!

"Let's meet Silvermist," Tink says. "Silvermist is a water-
talent fairy who can talk to babbling brooks. She is encouraging,
sympathetic, and quick to lend a hand!"

The fields and meadows of Pixie Hollow are filled with colorful flowers and plants of every type that bloom here year-round. Gentle garden fairies can revive wilted blossoms with a sprinkling of pixie dust. These fairies also take care of young bulbs, making sure they get off to a good start!

"Here we meet Rosetta," Tink says. "Rosetta is as pretty as the roses in her garden! She is nurturing and loves color, beauty, and sweet-smelling things."

It's impossible to be anything but bright-eyed and lighthearted in Sunflower Meadow! Filled with sunflowers, this is the home of the light fairies. The sunbeams streaming through the golden petals are dazzlingly beautiful. Here, light fairies play jump rope with beams of light and gather sunlight in buckets!

"In the meadows is Iridessa," says Tink. "Iridessa is a brilliant light-talent fairy. She creates and captures colorful rainbows!"

At Pine Tree Grove, you can get an up-close-and-personal look at Pixie Hollow's wildlife. Animal fairies take care of all the furry, fuzzy, and feathered creatures—and will even join in a game of leapfrog! Fairies' homes can be found right next to birds' nests and chipmunks' hideaways!

"Meet Fawn!" Tink says. "Fawn is an animal-talent fairy. She can talk to and comfort all the animals in Pixie Hollow. She is confident and energetic—a rough-and-tumble tomboy."

The best place to find fairies is at the Pixie Tree Dust Well, located in the Pixie Dust Tree at the heart of Pixie Hollow. At sunrise, every fairy goes there to get a daily dose of pixie dust. It's the perfect spot for fairies to catch up on gossip and talk about their plans for the day.

"I found Terence," says Tink. "Terence is a dust-keeper fairy. He makes sure each fairy gets just the right dose of pixie dust— not too much, not too little."

"One of my favorite places is the tinkers' workshop in Tinker's Nook. This is where tinker fairies carve acorn buckets, weave baskets, and fix wagons, pots, pans, and anything else that needs repairing. I am almost always here working on my newest inventions," Tink says.

"Most of Pixie Hollow is safe and carefree. But there are a few things to watch out for," Tink advises. "First, avoid Needlepoint Meadow, where the Sprinting Thistles grow. These tall, prickly weeds race around, trampling or poking anyone in their path! Second, beware of hawks! These fierce forest hunters can whisk away a fairy in an instant! And third, watch out for Vidia. She's the only fairy who can ruin someone's day with one mean remark."

Vidia is the fastest flying fairy in Pixie Hollow, and she knows it! She lives by herself in a sour-plum tree. She is known to be impatient, conceited, and annoyed by everyone!

There's so much to discover and explore in Pixie Hollow. You know the way—head toward the second star to the right, and fly straight on 'til morning. When you arrive, all your fairy friends will be waiting for you!

The End

Disney FAIRIES

Meet Tinker Bell

PIXIE HOLLOW BAKE OFF
Cupcake toppers included!

Pixie Hollow Reading Adventures
5 Books in 1!

Disney FAIRIES
THE PIRATE FAIRY

Wake Up, Croc!

Adventure at Skull Rock

Reusable Sticker Book
Over 80 stickers inside!

Meet Zarina the Pirate Fairy

The Chapter Book

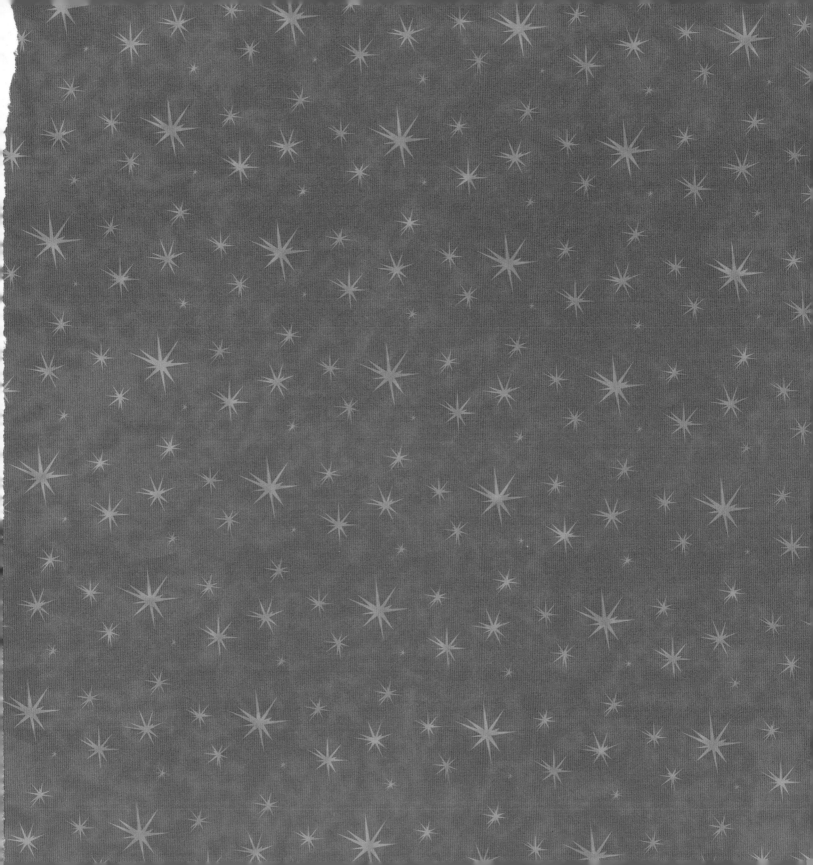

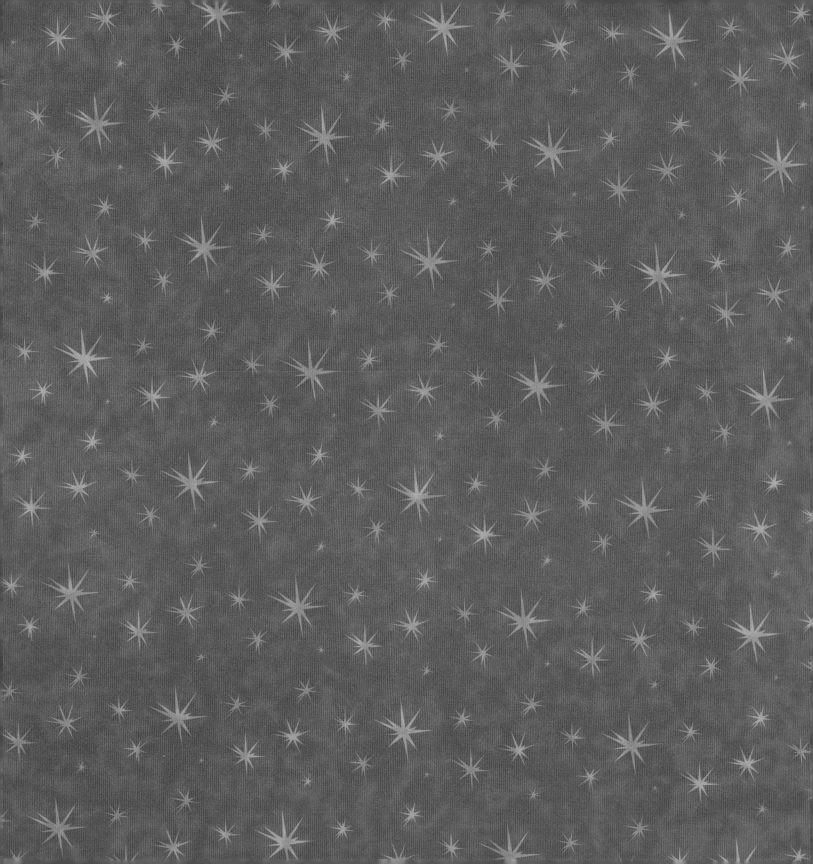